and the

Little Devil

First published in Great Britain 1987
This edition published in 2002
by Egmont Books Limited
239 Kensington High St, London W8 6SA
Published in hardback by Heinemann Library,
a division of Reed Educational and Professional Publishing Ltd
by arrangement with Egmont Books Limited
Text copyright © Penelope Lively 1987
Illustrations copyright © Valeria Petrone 2000
The author and illustrator have asserted their moral rights
Paperback ISBN 1 4052 0489 3
Hardback ISBN 0 431 06184 X
10 9 8 7 6 5 4 3 2 1
A CIP catalogue record for this title
is available from the British Library.
Printed and bound in the U.A.E.

Debbie
and the
Little Devil

PENELOPE LIVELY
Illustrated by Valeria Petrone

YeLLoW Bananas

To Gaby and Massimo
V.P.

Chapter One

THE FIRST TIME Debbie saw the devil he was
sitting on the end of her bed with one knee
crossed over the other, humming to himself
and prodding Debbie's foot with a long black
fork. The devil was about eighteen inches high
and as red as a hot coal. He had a long tail,
two neat horns on his head and little black
eyes. It was two o'clock in the morning.

Debbie sat up and said 'Stop poking my foot, do you mind!'

'Maybe,' said the devil. 'We'll see. I've got a job for you. You be a good girl and do what I say and we shall get on fine.'

'Are you a ghost?' asked Debbie.

'Certainly not! Nasty common things, ghosts. Upstarts. Ghost indeed!'

'Then what are you?'

'I'm a devil,' said the devil. He swished his tail and grinned. 'The real thing. Consider yourself lucky. Not many people get a look at me these days. Five thousand years old, I am!'

'I'm eight and a half,' said Debbie.

'Well, that's something to be going on with, I suppose,' said the devil. 'Now, let's get down to business. You know the cat next door? I want you to tie a tin can to its tail and then throw stones at it.'

'Certainly not!' said Debbie. 'That would be cruel and wicked and stupid and . . . and pointless.'

The devil scowled. He opened his mouth and blew a plume of bright red flame. 'I think it would be funny.'

'Well, I don't,' said Debbie, 'And don't smoke in my bedroom.'

The devil swished his tail again, which gave out a shower of little sparks, just like a firework. 'All right, then. Here's another idea. That old lady who lives opposite – you know, the one who walks with a stick. I want you to put a banana skin on her front doorstep so she'll step on it when she comes out and fall over.'

'You're *pathetic*,' said Debbie. 'You're so stupid you're pathetic. I'm almost sorry for you.'

The devil glared at her with his little black eyes and his tail fizzed away making blue and green and gold sparks.

'Spoilsport!' he snarled. 'You're hopeless, you are. No fun at all. Children aren't what they used to be.'

'I don't think I like you,' said Debbie.

'I'm not here to be liked,' snapped the devil. 'Just you wait and see.'

 At that moment Debbie's mother opened her bedroom door. The devil hissed and spat and blew another plume of flame and then he shrivelled up and vanished.

Debbie's mother came into the room and said she'd heard something – was there anything wrong? Debbie explained that there had been a small red devil sitting on the end of her bed, poking her foot and blowing fire at her. Her mother tucked her up again firmly and said, 'What a funny dream, dear. Now turn over and go to sleep again – it's the middle of the night.'

Then she went downstairs to check that she hadn't left the cooker on, because there was such a peculiar hot smell around the house, and when she had seen that all was well she went to bed again.

The next night the devil was back. Debbie woke up with a jump and there he was, grinning and humming and prodding with his fork. 'Go away!' she cried furiously.

'Shan't!' said the devil. 'We've hardly begun. Now listen to this. I want you to go downstairs and play around with some lighted matches so the house catches fire. Wouldn't that be fun!'

'You're horrible and nasty and *stupid*!' said Debbie. 'GO AWAY!'

'Sticks and stones may break my bones, but unkind words can't hurt me!' chanted the devil.

Debbie sat up. She reached for the glass of water by her bed and threw it at the devil as hard as she could. Debbie was rather a good shot so the glass hit the devil fair and square in the middle. It went straight through him and landed on the floor, where it broke. There was water everywhere.

The devil laughed and laughed. 'See!' Then he got smaller and smaller until he vanished and in the morning Debbie had to explain to her mother about the broken glass and the spilled water. She explained exactly and truthfully. Her mother was cross. She was cross about the broken glass but even more, she said, about making up silly stories.

Chapter Two

THE NEXT TIME the devil appeared was when Debbie was on her way home from school. There he was sitting on a wall at the end of her street. Nobody was paying any attention at all to him. A woman walked past him and the devil reached out with his fork and poked her in the side with it, and the woman slapped herself as though maybe she'd been stung by a wasp and walked straight on.

When Debbie reached him the devil said 'Wotcha!'

'I'm not talking to you,' said Debbie.

'But I'm talking to you,' said the devil. 'You won't get away with it like that. I'm older and wiser and cleverer than you are and I always win.'

'Bet you don't!' said Debbie, annoyed.

'Bet I do!' retorted the devil. 'Try me and see. What are you good at?'

Debbie thought. 'Jumping.' This was true. She'd won first prize in long jumping at the school sports and she was pretty good at high jumping too.

'Right!' said the devil. 'You see that pile of plastic rubbish bags there? Let's see who can clear that and land furthest on the other side. You first.'

Debbie stepped back and took a good run at the rubbish bags. She went flying over them but she'd gone at it a bit too fast and when she landed she tripped and came down on her knee. There was a nasty graze and quite a bit of blood. Trying not to cry, Debbie got up to watch the devil.

The devil rushed at the rubbish bags. When he was a yard away he jabbed his fork into the pavement and used it to give himself a huge push off. He came flying over and landed on his feet a yard further than Debbie. 'Easy!' he said. 'Ten out of ten to me. One out of ten for trying, to you.'

'You cheated!' howled Debbie. 'You used that thing of yours! You pole-vaulted! That wasn't fair!'

'Fair?' said the devil, 'Who's talking about fair? We're talking about winning. I told you I always win. Now you've got to do what I tell you or else. Go into the corner shop and nick some sweets.'

'I will not,' said Debbie. And she ran straight home where her mother plastered her knee but scolded her for fooling around in the street.

After that the devil really dug himself in at Debbie's home. Sometimes he woke her up in the night and at other times he'd suddenly appear, sitting up on the kitchen cabinet making faces at her or perched on the stairs or hanging from a tree in the garden. 'Whoo-hoo!' he'd say. 'Remember me?' Debbie's parents neither saw nor heard him. They walked straight through him. And Debbie was told off for talking to herself and being silly.

Chapter Three

THERE WAS WORSE than that, though. Things happened, when the devil was around. People dropped things and fell over and blamed each other and lost their tempers. One morning he stuck out his fork when Debbie's mother was bustling around the kitchen; Debbie's mother tripped up and dropped the tray she was carrying and scolded Debbie for getting in her way and everyone was cross with everyone else for the next half hour.

'That was your fault,' said Debbie to the devil, who was warming his toes on top of the cooker. 'You're beastly.'

'Sticks and stones . . . ' began the devil.

'Oh, BE QUIET!' shouted Debbie. 'I know all about that. But you won't always get it your own way, you'll see.'

'I always have,' said the devil, swishing his tail so that sparks flew all over the place. 'What's so special about you? I always win, remember. Who jumped furthest?'

'All right,' said Debbie. 'We'll try something else. And if I win you go away forever. Right?'

The devil swished and grinned.

'That's the bargain,' he said. 'I'm safe enough. What's a bit of a girl like you against someone five thousand years old who knows everything in the world.'

'Everything?' said Debbie.

'Absolutely everything,' said the devil.

'All right,' said Debbie. 'What does the Queen have for breakfast?'

'Fried snails,' said the devil promptly.

'She does not!'

'Prove it!'

'You're ridiculous,' said Debbie 'Very well then – what's black and white and read all over?'

The devil scowled and swished and sparked. His eyes flashed. 'Um . . . ' he said. 'A . . . The . . . Um . . .'

'A newspaper!' said Debbie triumphantly.

The devil hissed like a steam engine. He blew out a great tongue of flame.

21

'And what's the difference between an elephant and a post-box?' cried Debbie.

The devil glared. He opened and closed his mouth. 'An elephant . . .' he began, 'A post-box is . . . '

'Try posting a letter in an elephant and you'll find out!' shouted Debbie. 'And now tell me what's the highest mountain in the world? And who's the president of the United States of America? And how far away is the moon?'

But the devil had had enough (which was just as well since Debbie didn't know the answer to the last question herself). He huffed and puffed until he looked like a fat toad sitting there on the cooker. He sparked and flamed and then vanished with a pop, leaving behind the most dreadful smell of rotten eggs and burnt cabbage and drains. Debbie's mother telephoned for both the plumber and the electrician, neither of whom could find anything wrong, so there was more bad temper all round.

Chapter Four

AND THE VERY next day the devil turned up in the car, on the way to visit Aunt June. Debbie's father was driving and her mother was in the passenger seat and Debbie was in the back, and all of a sudden there was the devil too, sitting beside her with his fork propped up against his knees.

'You can't come to Aunt June's,' said Debbie.

'Try and stop me,' said the devil.

'What, darling?' said Debbie's parents, both at once.

'Nothing,' said Debbie, wearily.

The devil quite spoiled the outing. There he was, trailing around behind Debbie all day, making rude remarks, sitting on the sideboard all through dinner, poking the fruit in the fruit bowl with his fork – and none of the grown-ups knew a thing about him. He behaved very badly. He interrupted and jumped around the room and at one point he even started singing, in a high cackling voice that of course only Debbie could hear. Eventually she couldn't stand it any more.

'SHUT UP!' she cried.

'Debbie!' said her mother. And everyone stared at her and all she could do was mutter, 'I didn't mean you . . . ' which was no help at all. The devil perched on the windowsill and laughed.

'I'm not afraid of you, you know,' said Debbie to the devil on the way home. 'I'm just *bored* by you.' The devil was lolling on the back seat of the car, with his feet on the window ledge. His tail hung down against Debbie's leg. She gave it a push; it was like putting your hand right through a piece of red velvet.

'I don't exactly think you're a bundle of fun, either,' said the devil. 'As children go, you're a dead loss.'

'Then why hang around like this?'

The devil yawned. 'Because one's got a job to do.' And he went to sleep, snoring loudly.

Chapter Five

THE DEVIL WAS a bad loser, Debbie discovered.
He challenged her to game of Scrabble and
when Debbie started winning the devil turned
all the letters into black beetles. They ran about
the board and ruined the game.

'Don't *do* that,' said Debbie, 'That's my
Scrabble game Aunt June gave me for Christmas.
Now look at it!' The beetles ran round and round
the table and the devil sulked.

'Oh, you're just *babyish* . . . ' said Debbie.
'All right, I'll let you win, but get rid of those
beetles.' The beetles vanished and the letters
came back and the devil scored three hundred
and fifty-six and sat there grinning.

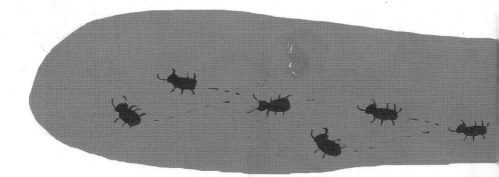

She beat him at cards, too. Snap and Rummy.
So the devil turned the cards into dead leaves
and Debbie's mother came into the room and
wanted to know what all that rubbish was
doing all over the floor. The devil, by then,
had whisked up onto the curtain rail and was
swinging by his tail, spitting fire.

'Have you been touching the matches, Debbie?' said her mother, sniffing.

When she had gone Debbie said to the devil, 'All right, then. You can win but next time I choose what we play, or I'm not playing at all.'

'You've got to play,' said the devil, 'That's what it's all about.'

'What do you mean?'

'It's what I do,' said the devil, 'I  come here and pick on someone and they have to play games with me till one of us wins. Except I always win,' he added quickly. And he made a nasty face at her.

'Suppose you don't?' said Debbie. 'I already proved you don't know everything in the world. I beat you at Scrabble. And cards too, except you cheat.'

31

The devil fizzed his tail around. 'I don't know what cheat means. One does what one does. I'm just better at doing things than you are.'

'We'll see about that,' said Debbie. 'Two can play at that game.'

'All right,' said the devil. 'Let's get serious, then. No more messing about. Best of three. And then you have to do what I say for ever and ever.'

'If you win,' said Debbie. '*If . . .* '

She looked hard at him and the devil squinted back with his squinny black eyes and sent out little forks of fire from his red mouth.

'And if *I* win . . .' said Debbie, 'then what?'

The devil spat and hissed. 'All right,' he said, 'all right. I'll stick to the rules. Such as they are. You win and I'll go.'

'Cross your heart?' said Debbie.

The devil laughed.

'All right, then – swear on that fork thing of yours.'

'Swear,' said the devil, 'And I can't get more honest than that. It was my dad's, that was, and his dad's before that.' He patted his fork fondly with one red paw. 'There! Sworn! But I'm wasting my time. I'll win. You'll see.'

'We'll see,' said Debbie.

They were in the kitchen. The devil hopped down from the back of the chair on which he had been sitting and rubbed his hands with enthusiasm.

'So . . . What shall we start with? How about a race? Simple flat race. From the back door to the end of the lawn and back.'

Debbie looked at him. She was more than twice as tall as he was; her legs were much longer. Wasn't it obvious that she would win? What was the devil up to?

'No funny business?' she said sternly.

'No funny business,' said the devil. His tail swished; sparks showered the floor.

I don't trust you, Debbie thought. I don't trust you one little bit.

They went out into the garden. 'Back doorstep is the start and finish post,' said the devil. 'Right?'

'Right,' said Debbie.

They lined up. 'One, two, three . . . go!' cried the devil.

Debbie sprinted. She was way ahead at once.

Just before she got to the end of the lawn she
looked back. There was the devil, pounding
away a couple of yards behind, his eyes flashing
and his tail whisking, looking like a huge spider.

Debbie turned at the rose bed and began to
sprint back. Halfway she felt a rush of air.
The devil flew past her, like a hot wind . . .
Whoosh!

And fly was exactly what he did. There on
his back had sprouted a pair of little black
wings. When Debbie got to the back doorstep

he was crouched down wriggling around. The
wings shrank and shrank and vanished into the
back of his neck.

'CHEAT! CHEAT! CHEAT!' shouted Debbie.
'You said no funny business.'

'Funny business?' replied the devil. 'What's
funny? I'm not laughing. Bad luck,' he added.

'Well tried and all that.' He rubbed his hands.
'One down, two to go. Now what? How about
some more jumping?'

'No,' said Debbie. 'It's my turn to choose.
We'll do throwing.' She knew she was a good
shot. 'We'll put a stick in the middle of the lawn
and see who can throw a quoit over it from
here. Best of three.' And before the devil could
say another word she had arranged the stick
and was handing him the quoit. 'You start.'

The devil scowled. You could see him
thinking away like mad. 'Go on,' said Debbie.
'You're not *scared*, are you? I thought you
always won?'

The devil flung the quoit. It flopped down a yard from the stick. Debbie threw; she was so jumpy she missed too. The devil grinned and took the quoit again. He threw . . . and the quoit went spinning past the stick. The devil jumped up and down and thrashed his tail on the grass.

Debbie aimed carefully. The quoit landed neatly over the stick. The devil, hissing now, ran to pick it up. He squinted at the stick . . . aimed . . . and threw. The quoit knocked the stick over and landed on the far side of it. The devil howled with rage.

'Last round!' said Debbie.
She took a deep breath
and threw, and plop! . . .
again the quoit landed fair
and square over the stick.
She looked at the devil and
the devil looked at her.

'Your go,' said Debbie.

The devil blew himself
out like a ball. His spidery
arm holding the quoit shot
out till it was twice its
length, like a piece of
pulled elastic. He hissed
and puffed and then he
threw . . . and missed.

'I WON!' cried Debbie.

The devil jumped around and fizzed till he
looked like a firework. 'All right!' he spat. 'One
all. Last round. And this time it's brain work.
No more of this silly sport stuff.'

'Right!' said Debbie.

'Maths,' said the devil. 'We'll go up to your room where nobody'll disturb us and have a maths competition to settle it.'

'How old did you say you were?' said Debbie.

'Five thousand.'

'And I'm eight and a half. So you've had . . . um . . . four thousand nine hundred and ninety-one and a half years more than I have to learn maths in.'

'Scared?' jeered the devil.

'No. I am not!' shouted Debbie.

They went up to her room and Debbie shut the door firmly. Downstairs, her mother called up, 'What are you up to Debbie?' and Debbie called back, 'Nothing, Mum. Just doing some homework.'

Debbie and the devil sat down at either side of the table. Debbie waited until the devil was looking the other way and then slipped her school calculator out of her jeans pocket and held it on her knee where he couldn't see it.

'We take it in turns to set the questions,' said the devil. 'First to answer wins the round. First to win two in a row is the outright winner. This is it! I start. Seven times eight!'

'Fifty-six!' they both said together.

'Eighteen plus six!' cried Debbie.

'Twenty-four!' snapped the devil, just ahead. 'One to me! Gotcha! My go. Two times three times four!'

'Twenty-four again!' shouted Debbie, almost before he had finished.

The devil blew out a great spout of flame. 'Right! Now let's see who's so clever . . . Last question. Quick!'

'Three hundred and forty-eight times five hundred and ninety-seven,' said Debbie loudly and slowly and clearly.

The devil's eyes gleamed. He spat some more flame. '*Now* who's being a bit too clever,' he said. '*Now* who's going to get what's coming to them! Um . . . three sevens are twenty-one, carry two, three nines are . . . '

Debbie's fingers tapped away. She glanced down. 'Two hundred and seven thousand seven hundred and fifty-six!'

The devil glared. He went on muttering and counting on his fingers. And then he gave a great howl of fury. He howled and jumped and gnashed his teeth. His tail whirled around, the whole room was filled with flying sparks. He spat flame so that Debbie had to duck down under the table. And then he started to get smaller. And as he shrank he howled . . .

a howl that trailed away as the devil himself
began to disappear. He got smaller and smaller
until there was nothing on the other side of the
table but a little red thing like a coal still
spitting and smoking. And then with a final
bleep and a flash he was gone.

Where he has gone is a secret. Whether or not he will come back nobody knows. As for Debbie, she was now one of the very few people to have tricked a devil, so she went down and ate a very large tea to celebrate.

KINGFISHER READERS

level **4**

Weather

Chris Oxlade

KINGFISHER

KINGFISHER

First published 2012 by Kingfisher
an imprint of Macmillan Children's Books
a division of Macmillan Publishers Limited
20 New Wharf Road, London N1 9RR
Basingstoke and Oxford
Associated companies throughout the world
www.panmacmillan.com

Series editor: Heather Morris
Literacy consultant: Hilary Horton

ISBN: 978-0-7534-3063-7
Copyright © Macmillan Publishers Ltd 2012

9 8 7 6 5 4 3 2 1

1TF/0512/WKT/UNTD/105MA

A CIP catalogue record for this book is available from
the British Library.

Printed in China

Picture credits
The Publisher would like to thank the following for permission to reproduce their material. Every care has
been taken to trace copyright holders. However, if there have been unintentional omissions or failure to trace
copyright holders, we apologise and will, if informed, endeavour to make corrections in any future edition
(t = top, c = centre, r = right, l = left):
Cover Photolibrary/Wessex; Shutterstock/Charles Miller; Pages 4 Shutterstock/Dimitry Shironosov;
5t Photolibrary/Ernest Washington; 5b Alamy/Alaska Stock; 7 Shutterstock/Hunor Focze; 8 Photolibrary/
Bill Bachmann; 9t Science Photo Library (SPL)/Martyn F. Chillmaid; 9b Photolibrary/Mike Berceanu;
11t Photolibrary/Galen Rowell; 12 Alamy/Enigma; 13t Shutterstock/Yaroslav; 14 Shutterstock/Daniel Loretto;
15 Shutterstock/Yuri4u80; 16 Photolibrary/Corbis; 17 Photolibrary/ Galen Rowell; 18 Shutterstock/Zibedik;
19t Shutterstock/Jostein Hauge; 19b Photolibrary/ Galen Rowell; 20-21 Shutterstock/Yoann Combronde;
21t Photolibrary/Horst Sollinger; 22 SPL/David Hay Jones; 23t SPL/NASA/JPL/CALTECH; 23b SPL/Paul
Wootton; 24 Alamy/Gautier Stephane/SAGAPHOTO.COM; 25t Corbis/Uwe Anspach; 25b Photolibrary/
Image Source; 26 Alamy/James Osmond; 27t Photolibrary/Eric Nathan; 27b Photolibrary/Markus Renner;
28 Photolibrary/Robert Harding; 29t SPL/Jim Reed; 29b Photolibrary/Walter Bibikow; all other images
from the Kingfisher Artbank.

Contents

What is weather?

What is the weather like where you are today? Is the Sun shining brightly or is the sky covered with clouds? Is it pouring with rain or is thick snow falling? Is the **wind** whistling around or is there no wind at all? Sunshine, clouds, rain and wind all make up the weather.

When the weather is sunny it is fun to play outside.

When it's wet you need a
raincoat, boots and an umbrella.

The weather affects
us almost every day. It
affects the clothes we
wear and the things we
can do. Should we take
an umbrella or a sun hat?
If it is sunny, we might go to the park instead of
staying indoors. But the weather is much more
important for people like farmers and sailors.
Their lives depend on the weather.

Fishermen often work at sea in very bad weather.

Air and the atmosphere

Satellite

Space shuttle

Aurora lights

Shooting stars

Weather balloon

Aeroplane

Weather layer

Air is all around you, all the time. You can feel it hitting your face when you run or ride your bike, or when the wind blows.

The Earth is covered by a layer of air called the **atmosphere**. The atmosphere stretches above the Earth for hundreds of kilometres, but the weather only happens in the bottom part of it.

This picture shows the things that happen at different heights above the Earth.

Temperature

The **temperature** of something is how hot or cold it is. The temperature of the air makes the weather feel hot or cold. We use a thermometer to measure the temperature of the air.

The atmosphere keeps the Earth warm like a blanket. It catches heat that comes from the Sun. The Sun heats the ground, and the ground heats the air above it. The weather on Earth would be much colder without the atmosphere.

This photograph, taken from space, shows the thin layer of atmosphere around the Earth.

What is the wind?

The wind is moving air. Sometimes it's a gentle breeze, sometimes it's a howling gale. Winds happen because heat from the Sun makes the air move about. When the Sun heats air near the ground, the air floats upwards. Cooler air flows in to take its place. This makes wind.

Sea breeze

On a sunny day at the seaside, warm air over the land rises up. Cool air moves from over the sea towards the land, making a breeze.

Measuring the wind

When we measure the wind, we measure how fast the air is moving in kilometres per hour. We also have to say in which direction the air is moving. For example, a north wind is a wind that is blowing from the north.

Wind vanes measure the direction of the wind.

Anemometers measure the speed of the wind.

Sometimes a huge area of warm air meets a huge area of cold air. Where the warm air and cold air meet, clouds form and rain falls.

Clouds forming above the Earth, photographed from space

Clouds

Wispy white clouds and lumpy black clouds look very different, but they are both made from millions and millions of tiny water droplets or **ice crystals**.

Cirrus clouds are wispy clouds high in the sky. They show the weather might be changing.

Water droplets and ice crystals are made when water in the air cools down. Water in the air is an invisible gas, called **water vapour**. There is always some water vapour in the air. It comes from water in the oceans and in the soil.

Strange clouds
Sometimes you see clouds with strange shapes in the sky. The clouds in this picture are called lenticular clouds. People sometimes think they are flying saucers!

Clouds come in all sorts of shapes and sizes. Some are fluffy, some are flat, and some are wispy. Some are low in the sky and some are very high. Different sorts of clouds bring different sorts of weather.

Cumulonimbus clouds bring rain, thunder and lightning.

Stratus clouds are flat layers of cloud that often bring rain.

Rain and snow

Rain and snow come from clouds. When the water droplets or ice crystals in clouds grow large enough, they fall to the ground.

Sometimes rain comes from water droplets in a cloud, but often rain comes from ice crystals that melt as they fall to the ground. Snow comes from ice crystals that reach the ground before they melt.

Water vapour cools and makes clouds.

This rain is made up of big drops of water. Heavy rain like this often causes **floods**.

Water **evaporates** from seas, lakes and rivers.

Snowflakes

Snowflakes are made from ice. They grow in very cold clouds. They start off as tiny ice crystals, and then get larger and larger. All snowflakes have six sides.

Water is always moving round between the land, the seas and the air. This movement of water is called the **water cycle**. This diagram shows how water moves around the water cycle.

Rain falls from the clouds.

Rainwater runs into rivers and back to the sea.

Water soaks into the ground.

Lightning and thunder

A flash of lightning is a spectacular sight. Lightning comes from giant storm clouds, called cumulonimbus clouds. They are full of water droplets and bits of ice that are flung up and down by super-strong winds.

Storm clouds can be 15 kilometres tall!

Inside a storm cloud, the water droplets and bits of ice crash into each other. This makes electricity in the cloud. When there is too much electricity for the cloud to hold, the electricity jumps to the ground making a giant spark. This is lightning.

Thunder

When a spark of electricity inside a storm cloud heats up the air suddenly, it makes a shockwave that rushes through the air. You hear the shockwave as a rumble of thunder.

Tornadoes and hurricanes

A spinning funnel of air comes down from a dark storm cloud. As it touches the ground, dust and objects fly up. Cars are thrown about like toys, and houses are torn to pieces. It's a **tornado**!

Tornado Alley

Tornadoes are common in the centre of the USA. Hundreds of tornadoes touch down here every year. The area is known as Tornado Alley.

Hail is made from lumps of ice that fall from storm clouds. Hailstones form when water droplets freeze together in very cold clouds. Most hailstones are smaller than peas, but sometimes they can be as big as coconuts!

Big hailstones like these can damage crops, buildings and cars.

This is the Atacama desert in Chile. It is the driest place on Earth.

It's raining fish!

In 2010, hundreds of small fish fell from a cloud on to the town of Lajamanu in Australia! Experts think a tornado sucked the fish up with water from a river.

Recording the weather

Every day, scientists all over the world record what the weather is like. They use instruments to measure the temperature of the air, how much rain falls, the speed and direction of the winds, how long the Sun shines for, and how much cloud covers the sky.

This scientist is copying data from an automatic **weather station.**

This map was made using information from a weather radar. The orange parts show areas over the oceans with the highest winds.

Weather balloons, **satellites** and **radar** all record information about the weather. Weather balloons carry measuring instruments into the atmosphere. Satellites take photographs of clouds from space. Radar can show where it is raining or windy.

A weather satellite high above the Earth, ready to take pictures

Weather forecasting

How do **weather forecasters** know what the weather is going to be like?

First, forecasters look at what the weather is like now. They get information about the weather from weather stations, weather balloons and satellites. Then they use powerful computers to help them work out how the weather will change. But weather is very hard to forecast accurately all the time. Sometimes even computers get it wrong.

A forecaster studies satellite photographs.

Weather computers

Weather computers use information about the weather now to work out what the weather will be like over the

next few days. They do this by doing billions of complicated calculations.

There are lots of different ways of finding a weather forecast. There are forecasts on the radio, on television, in newspapers and on the Internet. There are severe weather warnings when there is a danger of very strong winds or very heavy rain or snow.

This television presenter is explaining the weather forecast for the USA.

Patterns in the weather

The weather often changes from one day to the next day. But sometimes the same pattern of weather happens day after day. For example, in places near the Equator it always rains in the afternoon.

This is the same field in spring, summer, autumn and winter.

Most places have seasons. This means the weather is different at different times of the year.

Climate is the word used to describe the normal weather in a place. There are different types of climate around the world. Here are four climates:

- Polar: cold all year round, with long, very cold winters.

- Temperate: four seasons, with a cool winter and a warm summer.

- Tropical: hot and wet all year round.

- Desert (pictured): hot and dry all year round.

Climate change

Climates around the world change over time, and this is happening at the moment. Scientists think humans are to blame for today's climate change because we burn coal and oil, which puts carbon dioxide into the air. Climate change is causing glaciers and icebergs to melt.

Surviving in the weather

What do you do if the weather is really hot? Loose, thin clothes keep you cool. A hat and sun cream will protect you from the Sun's harmful rays. In very hot countries, people often live in stone houses, which help to keep them cool. They also stay indoors in the middle of the day.

Loose clothes keep the Sun's rays out but let cool air in.

This hole in the ground is a **tornado shelter**.

What would you do in a hurricane or tornado? When a hurricane is forecast, people stay indoors and cover their windows with boards to stop them breaking. In places where there are lots of tornadoes, people have underground tornado shelters in their gardens.

Animals and plants are specially **adapted** for the climate that they live in. For example, animals that live in cold climates have thick fur to keep them warm. Some animals, such as grizzly bears, hibernate (sleep over winter).

This cactus and prickly pear grow in the desert, where there is hardly any water.

Glossary

adapted Suited to the place where a plant or animal lives.

atmosphere The layer of air around the Earth.

climate Climate is the word used to describe the normal weather in a place.

Equator An imaginary line around the middle of the Earth.

evaporates When water turns to water vapour.

flood When a river breaks its banks and flows over dry land.

horizon The line where the land meets the sky.

hurricane A big storm that brings strong winds and heavy rain.

ice crystal A very small piece of ice.

poles The points furthest north and furthest south on Earth.

radar A machine that shows up where objects are in the far distance.

satellites Spacecraft that move around the Earth in space.

temperature How hot or cold something is.

thunder A loud rumble made by a flash of lightning.

tornado A spinning funnel of air.

tornado shelter A hole in the ground where people shelter from a passing tornado.

tropics An area around the Equator, where it is normally warm and rainy.

water cycle The movement of water between the atmosphere, the oceans and the land.

water vapour Water when it has turned into a gas.

weather balloons Big balloons that carry weather stations up into the atmosphere.

weather forecasters People who try to tell what the weather will be like in the future.

weather station A place where the weather is recorded.

wind Moving air in the atmosphere.

Index